Margaret Hillert's

I Like Things

A Beginning-to-Read Book

Illustrated by Jeff Hopkins

DEAR CAREGIVER,

The books in this Beginning-to-Read collection may look somewhat familiar in that the original versions could have been a part of your own early reading experiences. These carefully written texts feature common sight words to provide your child multiple exposures to the words appearing most frequently in written text. These new versions have been updated and the engaging illustrations are highly appealing to a contemporary audience of young readers.

Begin by reading the story to your child, followed by letting him or her read familiar words and soon your child will be able to read the story independently. At each step of the way, be sure to praise your reader's efforts to build his or her confidence as an independent reader. Discuss the pictures and encourage your child to make connections between the story and his or her own life. At the end of the story, you will find reading activities and a word list that will help your child practice and strengthen beginning reading skills. These activities, along with the comprehension questions are aligned to current standards, so reading efforts at home will directly support the instructional goals in the classroom.

Above all, the most important part of the reading experience is to have fun and enjoy it!

Shannon Cannon

Shannon Cannon,
Literacy Consultant

Norwood House Press • www.norwoodhousepress.com
Beginning-to-Read™ is a registered trademark of Norwood House Press.
Illustration and cover design copyright ©2017 by Norwood House Press. All Rights Reserved.

Authorized adapted reprint from the U.S. English language edition, entitled I like Things by Margaret Hillert. Copyright © 2017 Margaret Hillert. Reprinted with permission. All rights reserved. Pearson and I Like Things are trademarks, in the US and/or other countries, of Pearson Education, Inc. or its affiliates. This publication is protected by copyright, and prior permission to re-use in anyway in any format is required by both Norwood House Press and Pearson Education. This book is authorized in the United States for use in schools and public libraries.

Designer: Lindaanne Donohoe
Editorial Production: Lisa Walsh

LIBRARY OF CONGRESS CATALOGING-IN-PUBLICATION DATA
Names: Hillert, Margaret, author. I Hopkins, Jeff, illustrator.
Title: I like things / by Margaret Hillert ; illustrated by Jeff Hopkins.
Description: Chicago, IL : Norwood House Press, [2016] I Series: A
  beginning-to-read book I Originally published in 1982 by Follett
  Publishing Company. I Summary: "A young girl likes to collect and sort
  object such as buttons, rocks and stamps. She arranges objects by color,
  shape or size and shares in the fun with her parents and friends. Original
  edition revised with all new illustrations. Includes reading activities
  and a word list"-- Provided by publisher.
Identifiers: LCCN 2016001841 (print) I LCCN 2016022133 (ebook) I ISBN
  9781599538174 (library edition : alk. paper) I ISBN 9781603579889 (eBook)
Subjects: I CYAC: Collectors and collecting--Fiction. I Color--Fiction. I
  Size--Fiction. I Shape--Fiction.
Classification: LCC PZ7.H558 Iak 2016 (print) I LCC PZ7.H558 (ebook) I DDC
  [E]--dc23
LC record available at https://lccn.loc.gov/2016001841

288N—072016
Manufactured in the United States of America in North Mankato, Minnesota.

I like things.
Big things.
Little things.
Red and yellow
and blue things.

Look here.
Look here.
Here is something I like.
Something pretty.

Look what I can do.
Red, blue, yellow.
I can do it this way.
This is fun.

I can do it this way, too.
Big ones.
Little ones.

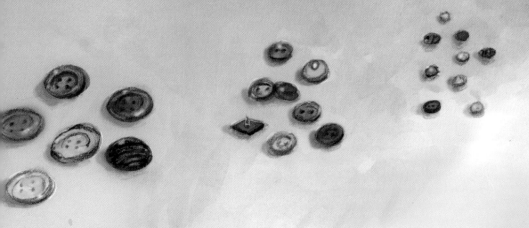

I can do it like this.
Oh, look at this.
This is a good way.

I can make something.
Something for Mother.
It is pretty.
Mother will like it.

Now here is something.
I like this, too.
Father helps me with this.

Oh, look.
Here are good ones.
Good ones for my book.

It is fun to do this,
but I have to work at it.
I find out things, too.
I like to do it.

Here is a good spot to
look for things.
I look and look.
What is here for me?
Guess, guess.

Now, look.
How pretty!
One can go here,
two here, and three there.

And I can do it
this way, too.
It is fun to play like this.

And here is something good.
I have things like this at
my house.

See this
and this
and this.

Look at the one in here.
See how this makes it look.
It looks big, and it looks pretty.

My friend comes to my house
to see what I have.
This is fun.

I have something that he wants.
And he has something I want.
I want it.
I want that one.

Things are good to have.
But we want something to eat, too.
Father will make something for us.

We will go out to play now.
We will look for things.
We will find things.
What fun we will have!

I like things.
Big things.
Little things.

Red and yellow and
blue things.
What things do you like?

Foundational Skills

In addition to reading the numerous high-frequency words in the text, this book also supports the development of foundational skills.

Phonological Awareness: The /th/ and /t̸h/ sounds

1. Say the word **thumb** and ask your child to repeat the /**th**/ sound.
2. Say the word **that** and ask your child to repeat the /t̸h/ sound.
3. Explain to your child that you are going to say some words and you would like her/him to show you 1 finger if the th sounds like /**th**/ (as in **thumb**) or 2 fingers if the **th** sounds like /t̸h/ (as in **that**).

thing	this	think	bath	three	path
they	them	moth	thread	thin	smooth
the	than	thorn	thirst	math	together

Phonics: /th/ and /t̸h/

1. Demonstrate how to form the letters **t** and **h** for your child.
2. Have your child practice writing **t** and **h** at least three times each.
3. Divide a piece of paper in half by folding it the long way. Draw a line on the fold. Turn it so that the paper has two columns. Write the words **thumb** and **that** at the top of each column.
4. Write the **th** words above on separate index cards. Ask your child to sort the words based on the **th** sounds that correspond to **thumb** and **that**.

Fluency: Echo Reading

1. Reread the story to your child at least two more times while your child tracks the print by running a finger under the words as they are read. Ask your child to read the words he or she knows with you.
2. Reread the story, stopping after each sentence or page to allow your child to read (echo) what you have read. Repeat echo reading and let your child take the lead.

Language

The concepts, illustrations, and text help children develop language both explicitly and implicitly.

Vocabulary: Nouns

1. Explain to your child that nouns are words for people, places and things.
2. Ask your child to page through the book to point out and name the people.
3. Repeat this by asking your child to do the same but pointing out and naming the things in the story.
4. Name the following nouns and ask your child to show 1 finger if it is a person; 2 fingers if it is a thing: buttons, sand, boy, jar, woman, friend, rocks, stamps, man, shells, girl.
5. Ask your child to name other familiar people and things while you show 1 or 2 fingers.

Reading Literature and Informational Text

To support comprehension, ask your child the following questions. The answers either come directly from the text or require inferences and discussion.

Key Ideas and Detail

- Ask your child to retell the sequence of events in the story.
- What are some of the things that the kids in the story like to collect?

Craft and Structure

- Is this a book that tells a story or one that gives information? How do you know?
- Do you think the friends like to go places to find things to collect? Why?

Integration of Knowledge and Ideas

- How would the girl take care of the things she collects?
- Do you collect anything? If so, what? If not, what would you like to collect?

WORD LIST

I Like Things uses the 67 words listed below.

This list can be used to practice reading the words that appear in the text. You may wish to write the words on index cards and use them to help your child build automatic word recognition. Regular practice with these words will enhance your child's fluency in reading connected text.

a	Father	I	play	us
and	find	in	pretty	
are	for	is		want(s)
at	friend	it	red	way
	fun			we
big		like	see	what
blue	go	little	something	will
book	good	look(s)	spot	with
but	guess			work
		make(s)	that	
can	have	me	the	yellow
comes	has	Mother	there	you
	he	my	things	
do	helps		this	
	here	now	three	
eat	house		to	
	how	oh	too	
		one(s)	two	
		out		

ABOUT THE AUTHOR Margaret Hillert has helped millions of children all over the world learn to read independently. She was a first grade teacher for 34 years and during that time started writing books that her students could both gain confidence in reading and enjoy. She wrote well over 100 books for children just learning to read. As a child, she enjoyed writing poetry and continued her poetic writings as an adult for both children and adults.

Photograph by Glenna Washburn

ABOUT THE ILLUSTRATOR Jeff Hopkins is a storyteller, educator, and children's book illustrator. He holds a BFA from the Rhode Island School of Design and a Masters in Education from Harvard University. Jeff has performed his "Pictures Come to Life" drawing/storytelling shows at museums all over the country. He is also a teaching artist for arts organizations in New York City, where he lives.